BEARD BURN

SHAW HART

Copyright © 2023 by Shaw Hart

www.shawhart.com

All rights reserved.

No part of this publication may be reproduced, transmitted, downloaded, distributed, stored in or introduced into any information storage or retrieval system, in any form or by any means, whether electronic, photocopying, mechanical or otherwise, without express permission of the publisher, except by a reviewer who may quote brief passages for review purposes. This book is a work of fiction. Names, characters, places, story lines and incidents are the product of the author's imagination or are used fictitiously. Any resemblances to actual persons, living or dead, events, locales or any events or occurrences are purely coincidental.

 Created with Vellum

WANT A FREE BOOK?

You can grab Sweets Here.
**Check out my website, www.shawhart.com for
more free books!**

*

You're going to like the burn...

Alba

Getting stranded in Clearwater is a disaster for me.

I have nowhere to stay, no money, and no friends.

Then I see the now hiring sign and I start to get my hopes up.

When I go in for my interview and meet Bishop, the grumpy giant who might just be my new boss, I think that maybe my luck is starting to turn.

Bishop

Hiring Alba would be a mistake.

For one thing, I think that my insurance rates would go up.

I mean, the girl can barely walk and talk without tripping or running into something.

A construction site is no place for a curvy little klutz like her.

No, I have somewhere better, somewhere safer, for her.

My place. Preferably in my bed.

Now I just need to figure out how to show her that I'm the man for her and that she belongs here in Clearwater with me.

ONE

Bishop

I CLIMB into my truck and slam my coffee into the cup holder. I'm already ready for this day to be over. I woke up late, raced through a shower that was at first way too cold, and then got way too hot. By the time I had the temperature just right, I was done with my shower and hurrying to get dressed and go.

I start the truck and hit the gas, peeling out of my driveway and down the nearly deserted backroads towards town. I finished up my part of the house we're building yesterday so I'm headed into the office to get caught up on paperwork. That's another reason why I'm ready for today to be over. I hate doing paperwork. I'd much rather be on a construction site, working with my hands and staying busy. That's the downside to being the boss, though.

I started Clearwater Construction right after I graduated from high school. I spent my Junior and Senior years dual enrolled in high school and local trade school. I knew that I wanted to get out of my parents' house and be on my own as soon as possible, and I worked hard to do just that.

I started my construction crew when I was nineteen and I've grown it over the last eight years to where I actually have a crew and more than just some friends helping me when they have the time.

My specialty is welding, which I do most of the time, though I can help out anywhere when needed. With one of my guys leaving, I need to hire someone to replace him, and fast. I've had a few job postings and ads out for the last week, but then I got busy with welding so today I'll be going through any applications I received.

I pull up in front of the Clearwater Construction offices and park. The town of Clearwater is just starting to wake up, and I give a few tight nods to people as I climb out of my truck and head inside. I'm not one to make a lot of small talk, and I know that some people in town probably think I'm a jerk or just a grumpy loner. They wouldn't be wrong.

My phone rings as I take a seat behind my desk, and I sigh as I answer.

"Yeah?"

"Still haven't replaced your secretary, huh?" My oldest friend asks with a laugh, and I groan.

"Shit, no. I forgot about that. I've been busy and focusing on replacing Jonas first," I tell Fisher.

"Well, you might want to get on that next. Your greeting would probably scare off any potential new clients," he advises me.

"I'll add it to my to-do list," I grumble, and he laughs again. "I don't need to worry about the new clients. We almost have more work than we can handle now."

"Damn, man. I was calling to see if you had time in your schedule in the next few months."

"You got a new project going?" I ask him.

Fisher and I grew up together here in Clearwater. We both wanted to get away from our parents, but Fisher wanted more than just getting away from them. He wanted to make something of himself and he's done that for sure. He opened his first resort in Mexico when he was twenty-one and it was a huge success. He's opened up ten resorts in the last seven years and is even more of a workaholic than I am.

"Yeah, it's nearby you too."

"Yeah? Where at?"

"I'm looking at Wolf Valley," he says.

"Where?" I ask, and he laughs.

"Yeah, I know. It's a small town, but they have a wolf reservation there. I've been working with the owners there to build a resort nearby so that people can stay in cabins and watch the wolves running by outside."

"Is that safe?"

"Yeah, a lot of the wolves there have been rescued and grew up there. They're friendly."

"Sure."

"They are!" He insists, and I smile.

"When are you starting?" I ask, opening up my calendar.

"I don't have definitive dates yet. I'm still waiting to finalize everything."

"Okay, well, I have time in three months or so."

"Alright, I'll keep you updated."

"Good."

I add a note to save some time for Fisher's new resort in my notebook and also to look up where the hell Wolf Valley is. I lean back in my chair, my hand running over my short beard, straightening the hair.

"What else is new with you?" He asks me, and I snort.

"Not a damn thing."

"Of course," he sighs, and I know he's smiling.

"What about you? You're the world traveler, billionaire. You should have some exciting stories," I counter.

This time, it's his turn to sigh, and I lean back in my chair.

"Not much. I've been working a lot. We just opened up the resort in Savannah, so there were a lot of finishing-up details."

Ah, that explains why he's working on the next resort. Fisher hates sitting still or having nothing to do. He's been like that since he was a kid. His mind was always working and he always had big dreams and a project going. Me, I always liked working with my hands so it made sense for me to go into construction.

"Alright, man. I've got to get back to work, but I'll talk to you soon," he says, and I can hear his assistant talking to him in the background.

"Sounds good. Talk to you later."

We hang up, and I turn on my computer and start to look through the handful of resumes that have been submitted. There are a few good candidates, and I'm about to start reaching out to them when my phone rings again.

"Yeah?"

"Hey, boss," Archer says, and I frown.

"Is everything okay at the job site?" I ask him.

"Yeah, just wanted to see if you were coming out here today."

"Do you need me to?"

"Yeah, some of the guys mentioned that they could use an extra hand today."

"Okay, I'll try to be there soon. I need to go through

these resumes and try to get the ball rolling on filling Jonas's old position."

"Alright, see you soon."

He hangs up. and I toss my phone on the desk and get back to work. I send off a few emails offering an interview and then start to pack up to head out to the job site. I'm standing to leave when the front door opens, and a woman falls at my feet.

"Sorry!" She apologizes as she starts to stand and I frown.

"No need to apologize. Are you alright?" I ask, and she nods.

Her mass of blonde hair is tangled in front of her face, and she brushes it back and smiles at me. It feels like someone just punched me in the gut, and all of the air leaves my lungs as I stare down at her angelic face.

"Hi, I'm Alba. I'm here for the job," she says, holding up one of the fliers that I had posted around town a few days ago.

"The job?"

Oh, hell no. There's no way that I'm letting this curvy little angel onto a construction site. She could get hurt. She could get hit on. I'm not letting either of those options happen on my watch.

This girl is mine. Now I just need to claim her.

TWO

Alba

THIS JOB IS JUST the thing that I need. As soon as I saw the job posting in the diner in town, I was sure that my day was about to look up.

I've been in Clearwater for a few days now, trying to find anyone who was hiring, with no luck. A lot of these little towns in Oregon aren't really hiring, which is a bummer for me because I really need a job. I'm getting really tired of moving around and the little savings that I had, quickly dwindled down to almost nothing.

My string of bad luck started two months ago when my apartment building almost burned down. It was an accident; I had tripped and knocked a candle over into the curtains. The fire got out of hand pretty fast, but I was able to put it out. I thought that everything would be alright, but my landlord didn't feel that way, and just like that, I was out of a place to live and lost most of my belongings.

I've been desperate to find a job and a new place to stay

ever since. That's why I'm here at Clearwater Construction, hoping to get hired to do construction even though I've never done that type of work, and I'm really not that good at working with my hands.

My parents would have laughed if I told them I was applying for a construction job. The thought makes me smile slightly, even as my heart aches from losing them. They passed away in a car accident three years ago, but the pain is still there. I don't think that it will ever really go away.

I've been on my own since they passed, trying to make my way in this world. I haven't been super successful at that so far, but I'm hoping that that's all about to change. I just need to land this job first.

I didn't make a great first impression, but maybe this giant lumberjack will take pity on me and still give me a chance.

I stare up at the handsome man and smile wider at him. He hasn't smiled at me yet, but I get the feeling this man doesn't smile at anyone.

Maybe he has smiled, but his beard is just covering it up, I try to tell myself.

He frowns down at me, and my smile starts to dim.

Guess not.

I don't know why, but when I had first seen him, a sense of peace had settled over me. I was sure that he was going to save me. I just felt like I had met my knight in shining armor... or I guess in shining flannel.

His dark brown hair was a little unruly like he was due for a trim. His dark blue eyes seemed intelligent and kind. He seemed like a safe person, like he was patient and understanding.

I've never had a crush before, but as soon as I saw him, I

finally got why so many girls my age are so boy-crazy. Except, I'm man crazy. And just about this man.

I wanted this man to be mine. I wanted to know that he was looking out for me, that he was keeping me safe. I wonder what it would feel like to curl up against his chest, to have his strong arms wrapped around me.

He looks tired and I long to smooth away his frown. I want to make him smile. I want to take care of him, to ease some of his burden and make him happy.

My thoughts start to turn dirty and I feel my face start to heat. I clear my throat, the paper that I'm still holding crinkling in my hands. I glance down at the job flyer and remember what I'm doing here.

"Are you still hiring for this position?" I ask him, holding the flyer up higher.

"You work in construction?" He asks flatly, and I wince.

"Well, no, but I'm a fast learner," I rush to say before he can tell me to get lost. "I'm sure that I could do it."

"No."

I blink.

Just like that, I deflate, and the flyer crumples in my hands as my last shred of hope is dashed.

"Why not?" I ask, determined to fight for a job since it's not like I have anything to lose.

"You have no experience, and a construction site is a dangerous place. I can't have a little thing like you tripping around it."

My shoulders slump, and I blink, fighting back tears. I have no money left, no apartment, and no job prospects.

What am I going to do now?

The man shifts on his big feet, and I swipe at my eyes.

"I could help out," I protest, and he shakes his head.

"No... but I have a different job for you," he says, and I hold my breath, eager to hear what it could be.

He doesn't elaborate, though, and my mind starts to race with what the job could be.

Maybe he needs help around here? Or at his place? Maybe in his bed...

I have no idea where that thought came from. I doubt that this man wants me for that, especially when he finds out that I'm a virgin. Still, now that the thought is there, I can't help but think about it.

"Wait!" I blurt out. "It's not like...something dirty, is it?" I ask him.

I'm not sure which one of us blushes more at my words.

THREE

Bishop

SOMETHING DIRTY?

I wish. Wait, is she thinking about me fucking her too?

I doubt it. What would this gorgeous angel want with a grumpy giant like me?

"No, not dirty. I need a housekeeper and someone to help out around here. It comes with a room at my house. I have a home office there too so you can take calls from the house or here."

"Okay, I'll take it!" She says, and she's back to smiling up at me, making my heart beat faster in my chest.

I love it when she looks at me like that. I need to make sure that I do something every day so that she will smile at me just like that.

Fisher and the guys on my crew have been teasing me that I need to do something besides work. I think that I might have just found the one thing that could tempt me to leave work and start spending some more time at home.

"Okay. Come on, I'll take you to my house and show you around. Then I need to get to a job site."

"Sounds good!"

She turns, practically skipping for the door, and I grab her arm when she trips over the threshold on her way out.

"Oh!" She squeaks as I hold her upright.

"Careful," I caution her.

She smiles up at me sheepishly and I vow to always keep her safe.

I never thought that I was the guy who was going to date or fall in love. No one in high school or this town had ever interested me and I just figured that I was always going to be happier alone. Two minutes around this girl though, and I think that I might have just found my forever.

"Thanks. What's your name?" She asks as we head out.

I lock the office door and follow her over to my truck and her beat-up car that's parked next to it.

"Bishop," I grumble, and she smiles.

"Nice to meet you, Bishop. I'm Alba."

"Alba," I say, wanting to feel her name on my tongue.

She smiles up at me and I try not to blush as I stare back at her.

"I'll follow you to your house?" She asks as she stops next to her driver's side door.

"Yeah."

We both climb into our cars and I drive slowly all the way back to my place. My eyes keep straying to the rear-view mirror to make sure that she's okay as she follows me.

We pull into the driveway and park. I hurry over to open her door and help her out of her car. She needs a new one. The tires are bald and she won't be safe to drive around town in that old rust bucket, especially in the winter. I make a mental note to research the safest cars and buy her one soon.

"Come on. I'll show you around."

I take her elbow and lead her up to the front door.

"I'll make you a key today," I tell her as I unlock the door and motion for her to go ahead of me.

"I love your place," she says as she looks around.

There isn't much to see. I built this place a few years ago, but I haven't done much to really make this place a home. It's still pretty bare in here.

"Thanks."

"Did you build it yourself?" She asks me, and I nod.

"Yeah, I bought the land a couple of years ago and then started working on it. It took a while, but I finished it like two years ago."

She nods, looking around the living room and then heading into the kitchen.

"The home office, kitchen, and living room are down here. Bedrooms are upstairs so you can take whichever one you want. Where are your things? I can help you move them in here later today."

"I don't really have much. It's all in my car," she says vaguely, and I frown.

I saw her car. There were only two or three small suitcases in there.

That's all she has?

"That's it?" I ask her, and she nods.

"There was, um," she starts as she stops in the kitchen. "There was a fire in my last apartment, and I lost a lot of my things."

"I'm sorry to hear that," I tell her, and she nods.

"It was pretty scary. It all happened so fast."

"You were home?" I ask, my heart racing out of control.

Jeez, she could have died.

I don't like that thought. Not one bit.

"Yeah, I actually, um, I started the fire," she admits, wincing slightly.

"You started a fire," I state flatly, and she nods.

"It was an accident! I tripped and knocked a candle over into the curtains. They caught on fire, and then by the time I found the fire extinguisher, my bedroom was on fire, too. I was able to put it out and all, but I lost my things and my apartment."

"I'm glad that you're okay."

"Me too," she says weakly.

She seems relieved that I'm not holding the fire against her, and I wonder what happened with her landlord and all of that to have her so spooked.

My phone rings, and I know that it's the guys.

"I need to get to work, but you can make yourself at home. I'll be home in a few hours, and we can go over tasks and stuff then. Here's my phone number if you need anything," I say, writing down my number on a scrap piece of paper in the kitchen.

"Should I make dinner?" She asks, and I nod.

"Sure, that would be great. I'll be home about five."

"Okay."

She follows me back to that front door and I force myself to smile and nod goodbye at her and head back to my truck.

I hate leaving her home alone. I want to get to know her better. I want her to get to know me. I want her to want me.

I hit redial on my missed call and I'm surprised when it's Fisher that picks up.

"Hey, everything alright?" I ask him, and he hums.

"Not really. I wanted to let you know that there's been a

set back on the Wolf Valley project," he says, sounding annoyed. "I didn't want you to hold off on booking someone else."

"Okay. Anything that I can help with?"

"No," he growls, and I wonder what has him so worked up.

"I hired someone," I tell him.

"That was fast."

"She's a klutz," I ramble.

"That seems... like a bad choice for an employee on a construction site," he says carefully.

"She's not working for my company. Well, she's going to be my new secretary and housekeeper."

"You hate people being in your space. Why did you hire a housekeeper?" He exclaims.

"I panicked," I admit.

"Why?"

"She's beautiful."

Silence greets that statement. Neither Fisher nor myself have ever been interested in women, so this is probably a shock to him.

"So, you hired her to work for you."

"I didn't want her to leave, and she looked so sad."

"Well, good luck with that."

"She burned down her last apartment," I blurt out, and he snorts out a laugh.

"Well, good thing you can build houses!" He says with a big laugh.

"I hate you."

That just makes him laugh harder.

"Watch it. One day you're going to meet someone, and I can't wait to give you shit then, too," I warn him.

I pull up to the construction site and wave at the guys as I grab my things.

"I'm at the site, so I have to go. I'll talk to you later," I say.

"Count on it," he tells me and I hang up before he can say anything else.

I sigh as I climb out of my truck and get to work.

FOUR

Alba

I CAN'T HELP but watch the clock as I make dinner. Heck, who am I kidding? I've been staring at the clock, willing time to go by faster, ever since Bishop left. I explored the house and spent way too much time in his room, running my fingers along his clothes and bed. I may have spent a few minutes picturing Bishop and me in his big bed, but as soon as I felt like I was overheating, I had left and moved on to the next bedroom.

I ended up picking that room as mine, and I hauled in my two suitcases and put my things away. That hadn't taken very long since I didn't have much. I took a quick shower, pulled on clean clothes, and then decided to get started on dinner.

Bishop didn't have a whole lot in his fridge, but I found some hamburger and spaghetti sauce, so I decided to make spaghetti and meatballs. I loved to cook. I used to do it all of the time with my mom before she passed. I guess over the last few years, I stopped doing it that much. It wasn't as much fun when I was just cooking for myself.

The meatballs are simmering in the sauce, and I'm about to drain the spaghetti when I hear a car pull up outside. My heart starts to race, and I smile as I see Bishop climb out of his truck and head up to the front door.

I school my features as he comes inside, but when his dark blue eyes meet mine, I feel my face start to heat in a blush.

Man, I really need to get this crush under control. I can't have him knowing that I'm fantasizing about him like that.

"Hey, how was work?" I ask him as I clear my throat and move to drain the spaghetti.

"Good. I'll get that," he says, rushing over to the kitchen to take the hot pot from me.

"Oh, thanks," I say in surprise, and he gives me a tight smile as he drains it for me.

I move to set the table and smile to myself as we move around the kitchen in perfect sync. I've missed this. I didn't realize how lonely I had gotten traveling around by myself.

I used to live with a friend, Elizabeth, but when I got kicked out, she decided not to come with me. I can't really blame her. It's not like I had a plan or another place to live all lined up. I had lost my work-from-home job after the fire too, so I didn't even have a way to pay rent. Still, it would have been nice if she had come with me.

Bishop unbuttons his flannel shirt and pulls it off. My mouth drops open slightly, and I watch in rapt fascination as he tosses it onto the couch.

I know that most people would be more attracted to a clean-shaven man in a suit and tie, but seeing Bishop in a white t-shirt and pair of jeans, with his beard and dark hair is the hottest thing to me. There's something so rugged and virile about it that, for the first time in my life, I'm getting turned on.

He comes my way, and I swallow hard, staring at him wide-eyed as he approaches.

"Let me get your chair for you," he says, pulling out my chair.

Sexy and he has manners?

I want to fan myself, but I resist and drop down into the chair. I know I must be blushing, but I try to play it off as he takes a seat across from me.

"How was your day?" Bishop asks me as we make our plates.

"Good. I put my things away," I tell him, and he nods.

I watch as he takes a bite of dinner and hold my breath to see if he likes my cooking. He moans slightly and quickly goes back for another bite. I grin to myself as I dig into my food.

"How long have you lived in Clearwater?" I ask him as we eat.

"All of my life," he says.

"That's nice. I've been living all over. My dad was in the military, so we moved around a lot when I was growing up. I was in San Francisco before I came here," I tell him, and he nods.

"Did you like it? I never cared much for big cities," he says.

"It was nice how convenient it was to run out and grab something, but I didn't like all of the traffic or the rent prices," I say with a laugh.

"That was what I hated too. I was too impatient to sit in traffic for hours every single day. It's why I never left Clearwater. I went to visit my friend who lives in Los Angeles and hated it. I vowed to never go back. I don't know how he can do that every single day."

"I bet there's never traffic here."

"Never," he says.

He finishes off his plate, and I smile as he goes back for seconds.

"What made you choose construction?" I ask when he sits back down.

"I always liked working with my hands and welding, electrical, plumbing, all of it just made sense to me. I was always good at it. Plus, not having to go to college to get a degree was a bonus."

"I didn't go to college either," I admit.

"You didn't like school?"

"No, I would rather be out doing other things than taking notes or classes I wasn't really interested in. I've taken a few classes at some local community centers, so I'm pretty good at accounting, playing guitar, doing yoga, and doing massage therapy," I tell him with a laugh.

"That's a pretty wide array."

"I just signed up for stuff that sounded interesting," I say with a shrug.

"That's cool. I always thought it would be cool to learn an instrument, but I never made the time to learn."

"Maybe I could teach you. Or we could try to find a class or teacher in town."

"Maybe," he agrees.

We finish eating and I carry everything over to the counter to start cleaning up. Bishop helps me, and we work together as a team to clean up.

He winces as he bends over to load the dishwasher and I frown.

"Are you okay?" I ask him, stepping closer.

"Yeah, just a little sore."

"Here, let me see," I tell him, taking his hand and leading him back to the kitchen chair.

He obliges me and sits. I push him forward so that I can reach his back better. I run my fingers over his back, feeling his muscles.

"You have a lot of knots right here," I say, pressing on one of them.

"Hmm," he grunts and I press harder.

"Let me know if I'm hurting you."

He snorts and then groans as I use my thumbs to work out the knots.

"Fuck that feels good," he moans and I smile.

I never pursued becoming a masseuse because I didn't think that I would like working on people all of the time. I like taking care of Bishop though. There's something about him that just connects with me. It's like he's my other half.

I work in silence, smoothing out the muscles in his back before I move to his neck and then shoulders.

"Have you ever gotten a massage before?" I ask him and he shakes his head.

"No, it never seemed like my thing."

"Too girly for you? Did your mom get massages?"

"I doubt it. We never had a lot of money growing up."

"We didn't either. I remember my mom saving up for months to take me to get my nails done for prom my senior year," I tell him with a smile. "It meant a lot to me."

"She sounds like a good mom."

"She was. She was the best."

"And your dad?"

"He was great too. He was more serious than my mom. He loved reading and he knew so many different random facts. He used to read me all of my bedtime stories. What about you?"

"My parents weren't great. Neither of them were ever going to win parent of the year," he tells me and my heart hurts for him.

"I'm sorry to hear that."

He shrugs, those big shoulders rising and falling easily now.

"It's fine. I moved out of their house as soon as I was able to and worked hard to never have to go back there. My desire to get away from them is what helped me to grow Clearwater Construction so fast."

"I'm glad that something good came out of it."

He smiles over his shoulder at me and I smile back.

I'm rubbing down his forearm when a crack of lightening sounds from outside, and I jump.

"Is it supposed to storm tonight?" I ask Bishop, my voice shaking.

"I think so. Why?"

I swallow hard. I hate storms. I have ever since I was a kid, and we lost power for three days. I've hated storms and the dark ever since.

"Alba? Are you okay?" Bishop asks, and I realize that I'm close to hyperventilating.

"I hate thunder and lightning. I hate the dark," I whisper.

Another bolt of lightning flashes across the sky, and I jump, banging my elbow on the counter behind me.

"Whoa! Easy," he says, pulling me into his arms. "It's okay. I've got you."

The lights flash in the kitchen, and my grip on Bishop tightens.

"Let me see if I can find a candle or a flashlight or something," he tells me, and I cling to him.

He starts to shuffle out of the kitchen, and I remain glued to his side, my eyes locked on the windows as we pass them.

He heads into his office and starts to open a few drawers, but there's nothing there. We head upstairs and I'm basically glued to him at this point.

I follow him into his room and shriek as thunder sounds, loud and imposing outside. He digs around in his bedside table and pulls out an old flashlight. My hopes soar, but when he turns it on, the light flickers and then stays off.

"It probably needs new batteries. I don't think that I have any, though."

"Oh-h, okay," I say, my teeth chattering.

"Shit, Alba. It's okay, baby. I'll... I'll start a fire and turn the heat up. You can sleep in my room with the fireplace tonight."

I nod, too scared to try to protest taking over his bed.

"I'll be right back," he promises me and I let him go reluctantly.

He takes off, rushing downstairs. I hear the backdoor open, and I peek out the window to see him running out into the rain and over to a covered wood pile. He disappears under the shed, and my breath stalls in my lungs until he comes running back out with some logs in his arms.

His footsteps are heavy as he jogs back upstairs and into his room.

"It's okay," he says, his eyes filled with worry.

I nod wordlessly as he starts to build a fire. I take a seat on his bed, trying to calm my racing heart as he lights a match and the fire starts to crackle.

"I'm just going to turn the air on so that it doesn't get too hot in here."

I nod again as he disappears back downstairs. My heart has started to stop racing out of control by the time he comes back into his room, and I finally notice that he's drenched, his white shirt transparent now and molded to his chest and muscles.

My mouth dries out at the sight of all of his muscles.

So. Many. Muscles.

His shirt clings to his pecs, and my body starts to heat as I stare at him. I can make out the smattering of dark chest hair and the ridges of his six-pack as the wet material clings to him.

I want to lick him.

I'm not sure where that thought comes from and it startles me and has me blinking out of my dirty thoughts.

"You can sleep here," he tells me as he pulls down the sheets for me.

"I don't want to take your bed from you," I protest weakly.

"It's fine. I'll sleep in the spare room."

"No!" I blurt. "Stay here. Please."

He studies me for a moment, and I wonder if he can see how desperate I am not to be alone right now.

"Please," I say again.

"Okay," he says, and I let out a breath of relief.

The storm is still raging as we start to get ready for bed. I dash into my room and grab some pajamas before I head back into his room. The power is starting to flicker and I don't want to be alone in case it goes out.

Bishop is in the bathroom, so I hurry to change and climb into his bed. He comes out a moment later in his pajamas and I watch him climb into bed beside me.

As soon as he lays down next to me, a new feeling washes over me.

Arousal.

Sexual tension fills the room and I'm too afraid to look at him.

What if this feeling is just on my side? That would be so embarrassing. Besides, I can't lose this job. I need it.

We lay in silence, both of us staring at the ceiling, and I beg for sleep to claim me. It's a long, long time before it does though.

FIVE

Bishop

I'VE BEEN rock-hard and distracted all day.

Waking up with Alba plastered against me was amazing. Her lush curves had felt perfect pressed against me, and it had taken everything in me not to roll her under me and make her mine. I had held back, remembering that she was only in my bed because she was frightened of the storm. She was looking to me for comfort, not to ravish her.

Unfortunately.

I pulled myself from bed reluctantly and left Alba sleeping as I took a shower and got dressed. I'm supposed to be back on the job site today to help out with finishing up a few things, but all I want to do is crawl back into bed with my girl and spend the day with her.

I head into the kitchen to make some coffee and scrawl out a note to Alba, letting her know that I'll be back for dinner but to call me if she needs anything. I hope that she does. I would love any excuse to get back home to her.

"What's gotten into you, boss?" Archer asks as he takes a seat next to me in the upstairs bedroom.

"Nothing," I growl, and he huffs out a laugh.

"There has to be something. You've been snapping at everyone all morning," he says, passing me a bottle of water.

I twist off the cap and chug half of the bottle before I answer him.

"There's this girl," I start, and he grins at me.

"I knew it!" He crows, and I glare at him.

"Shut up," I grumble.

I can hear the other guys working below us. We should be able to finish up this cabin by early next week, and I try to remember my schedule to see if I can take some time off to spend with Alba then.

"Who is she?" He asks me.

"Her name is Alba. I hired her yesterday to be my housekeeper and secretary."

"Okay, but..." he says, and I scowl at him.

"But what?"

"But you want her."

"Yes," I nod, and he grins.

"Have you asked her out yet?"

"No, it's too soon."

"Too soon? You're asking her out not to marry you," he says with a laugh.

An image of Alba walking towards me in a white dress fills my head, and my heart kicks hard. I want that. I want her to be mine in every way.

"It's complicated. I hired her... and she's living with me."

"Just go home tonight and flirt with her, feel her out, ya know?" He asks, and I frown.

"I don't know how to flirt," I admit.

"Well, just do the opposite of what you do every single day," he advises, and I flip him off. "No, seriously, just show her you're interested in her. Ask her questions about herself, find out what she likes and doesn't like, all of that."

He makes it sound easy, but I've never been the best conversationalist. I'm gruff and can be abrasive, but I can't be like that with my Alba.

"I'll try," I tell Archer, and he nods.

He claps me on my shoulder as he stands and heads downstairs to get back to work. I do the same, but my mind keeps straying to how I can flirt with Alba and try to win her over.

She's comfortable around me. I mean, she must be, right? She came home with me to start working yesterday when she barely knew me. She slept with me when she was scared, so she must see me as a safe person.

I work for a few more hours before I hear the guys packing up to head home. I'm almost done with my portion, so hopefully, I'll just have to come back tomorrow. Then I can head into the office with Alba for a day or two. It will be nice to have some more one-on-one time with her.

I pack up my things and wave goodbye to a few of the guys as I climb into my truck and head home.

I wonder if she's been missing me too. I wonder what she made us for dinner today.

I pull up in front of the house and hurry inside. The house smells good, and my stomach growls as I toe off my boots and head into the kitchen. My mouth waters as I see Alba bent over the oven, and my fingers itch to reach out and grab her.

"Smells good in here," I compliment her as I wash my hands.

"Thanks, I made my favorite comfort food."

"What's that?"

"Chicken tetrazzini. It's this cheesy, creamy spaghetti dish with chicken, and I made biscuits to go with it."

She beams as she shows me the dish, and I can't help but smile back at her.

"Looks great. Can I help with anything?"

"I just need to set the table."

"I'll do that," I tell her as I move to grab two plates and some forks.

She sets the casserole dish on the table and moves to grab the flaky biscuits as I grab us each a glass.

I never thought that I would like this domestic stuff. I always thought I was better off alone, but when I saw Alba, everything changed. I like how intimate it feels to move around the kitchen with her. I like having her in my space. I just like her.

"What did you do today?" She asks me as we sit down to eat.

I remember Archer's words about getting to know her better, and I know that I need to make a real effort to flirt with her now.

"I was just finishing up some stuff. I think I'll have to go back to the site tomorrow, but then I'll be able to take you back into the office and get you set up. I should be able to forward calls to your cellphone so you don't really have to go into town if you don't want to. You can use the home office here instead."

"Are you sure?"

"Yeah, I'll show you around and get you set up in the next day or so."

"Okay," she smiles, seeming excited to be able to get to work.

"What did you do today?" I ask her, trying to change the subject to her.

"I went into town and went grocery shopping. We didn't really have much here," she says with a sweet smile.

"I'll reimburse you. I'll have to get you a credit card to use for purchases."

"Oh, it's alright. I really just grabbed a few things. I think the total was less than twenty dollars."

I know that she was low on funds when I hired her. I want to ask her if she used her last twenty dollars on stuff to cook for me, but I bite my tongue.

"I'll pay you back, Alba," I tell her.

She nods and takes a bite of her food. She seems uncomfortable talking about money so I decide to change the subject. I know I need to talk to her about her salary, but I won't do that right now and ruin the mood.

I take a bite of my food, stalling for time. It's delicious, just like her spaghetti and meatballs last night, so I decide to ask her about cooking.

"Do you like to cook?" I ask her, and she grins.

"I love it. I used to do it all the time with my mom growing up."

"Is this one of her recipes?"

"Yeah, she taught me a ton of recipes. It was always fun to come up with new ones with her, too."

"Do you two still cook together?" I ask, and her smile falls.

"No, my parents passed away in a car accident a few years ago," she says softly, and I swallow hard.

"I'm sorry, Alba. That must have been hard."

"It was. Some days it still is," she admits.

We eat in silence for a moment and I decide to try to change the subject.

"How are you liking Clearwater? You said that you hadn't been in town for very long. I'll have to give you a tour around the place," I offer.

Does that count as a date? Maybe I can take her out for dinner, too. Then it has to count as a date.

"Sure, that would be great."

She's back to smiling, and I relax.

We finish eating at the same time and I help her carry the dishes over to the counter. She starts putting the food away while I start on the dishes.

"Oh, I can get those," she protests, but I shake my head.

"I'll help. I don't mind."

She comes to stand beside me and starts to dry the dishes. It's nice being so close to her, but it also has the arousal from this morning coming back in full force.

She smells so good, like sugar cookies, and it has my mouth watering for a taste.

"How about I take you out to dinner tomorrow?" I offer, and she smiles.

"Are you going to take me on that tour too?"

"Whatever you want," I promise her.

"Alright," she agrees, and I want to cheer.

I have a date with Alba.

"Great," I grin, and she blinks.

"You have a beautiful smile," she compliments me, and I want to grab her and kiss her.

"You have a beautiful everything," I blurt out before I can stop myself.

She flushes at my words, but she looks happy with the compliment.

She turns to put away a plate, and I finish with the dishes and wipe down the counters. When she turns around, she trips over her own feet, or maybe I scared her with how close I am. She starts to tumble forward, and I reach out, grabbing her hips and pulling her against me. My grip on her tightens as her lush curves press against me. I try to tell myself that I'm just trying to make sure she's steady on her feet and safe, but even after a minute, I can't seem to force myself to let her go.

We're face to face, and I think we both stop breathing as we stare into each other's eyes.

"Bishop," she whispers, and I swallow hard.

This is it. This is my chance, my moment with her.

I close the distance between us and seal her mouth with mine.

SIX

Alba

I STARE at Bishop as his head dips. My hands are clammy with nerves as I wait for him to kiss me. I lick my lips, and I can feel his warm breath as it fans over my face. His eyes close, and mine flutter closed, too, and then his mouth is on mine.

My first kiss.

I'm not sure what I'm doing, and I freeze at first, feeling foolish.

But then Bishop groans, combing his fingers through my hair and tilting my head up to deepen the kiss. His lips move against mine, coaxing breathy whimpers from somewhere deep in my chest. He licks his way into my mouth, his tongue dragging against mine slowly, seductively, as if he's savoring everything about this moment. His beard tickles my skin and I shiver as he kisses me harder.

I fist his shirt, pulling him closer as I get lost in him. Bishop tightens his hold on my hair, angling me just so, then he devours me. His other hand slides up and down my curves, leaving a trail of fire in its wake that has me burning hotter and hotter.

We make out until we're both out of breath. My neck is starting to hurt from the angle, and I wince, rubbing the back of my neck as I suck in a much-needed breath of air.

"So damn sexy," he groans, dipping his head to my neck. Bishop kisses and nips his way up the slender column while his big, strong hands take over rubbing the back of my neck.

I moan, and I'm not sure if it's from his kisses, the way his fingers are working my muscles or both.

His lips find mine again, and I lean against him, wanting to feel his strong body against me. My knees shake with the intensity of his kiss, his touch, his obvious need for me. I can feel the thick length of his erection pressing against my stomach, and I start grinding against him without thinking about it.

I need him.

After what feels like forever and still not long enough, Bishop breaks our kiss, resting his forehead on mine.

"Holy shit, baby," he says, breathless.

I grin at his pet name for me.

"Yeah, I know," I say with a light laugh.

"Alba, we don't have to do anything," he starts, and I laugh again.

"You can't get me all turned on and then leave me like this," I complain, and he looks relieved.

"I would never," he swears as he gathers me up in his arms.

He gives me another kiss, this one a lot more chaste, as he sweeps me up in his arms and takes off for the stairs.

"Where are we going?" I ask, kissing his neck.

"My room. Our room," he corrects, and I smile against his skin.

I like the sound of that, of us having a room together, or us sleeping together every night.

We head into his room and he stops next to the bed, letting me slide down his body to my feet.

"You're running this, baby. You want me to stop; you just say the word and I'll stop. I promise," he tells me, and I nod.

I won't be telling him to stop. I want him too badly.

"I want you," I promise him, and he nods.

He reaches for me, and I let him pull the hem of my shirt up and over my head. Nerves hit me as soon as the shirt drops by our feet. I've never been naked in front of anyone before, and I'm afraid that Bishop won't like me or want me once he sees me without my clothes on.

"So beautiful," he says almost reverently, and my head snaps up to see what he's talking about.

"Me?" I blurt when I see him staring at my body.

"Of course. God, Alba, you're the sexiest thing I've ever seen. I've wanted you from the moment that I saw you."

My body warms at the compliments. I've never had that before. Most guys always paid more attention to my friends than me. I've never been hit on or even looked at twice before.

"You're gorgeous, baby."

His hands land on my hips, and I shiver at his hot touch. His fingers trail softly along my skin until he reaches the button of my jeans, and we both seem to hold our breaths as he pops the button and pulls the zipper down.

He looks up at me, and I know he's making sure I'm okay with what's happening.

"Don't stop," I beg him, and he smirks slightly.

"I won't. Not until you're hoarse from screaming my name."

I almost moan from his words alone. He pushes my jeans and panties down my legs, and I kick them to the side. I'm left standing before him in just my bra, and Bishop reaches for that next, unhooking the clasp and tossing it onto the floor with the rest of my clothes.

"Your turn," I tell him, and he hurries to strip off his clothes.

I giggle at his eagerness, and he smiles at me as he tosses his jeans to the side. I can feel my face flushing as I let my eyes roam over him. He looks like he's cut from marble and I've never seen so many muscles before.

His cock is hard and pointing straight at me. It looks huge, and I swallow hard as I wonder how that thing will ever be able to fit inside of me.

"Come here," he says in a low, husky voice, and I move towards him until we're toe-to-toe.

Then Bishop is bending down and picks me up easily. I love that he can do that, but I don't have time to focus on how he makes me feel delicate. He drops me in the middle of the bed, and I laugh as he comes down over me, caging me in with his body. My legs spread, going to either side of his hips, and I stare up at him as he looms over me.

His lips drop down to claim mine, and I twine my arms around his neck as I get lost in him again. He rolls to the side, and his hands start to explore my body. His touch leaves goosebumps in their wake, and I shiver against him.

"I need to taste you," he groans as he trails kisses down my neck, and I nod.

"Yes... taste me," I beg.

He kneels between my legs, and his hands cup my breasts, molding the soft mounds in his hands. He rolls one of my nipples between his fingers, and I suck in a sharp breath as I feel an echoing pang of arousal between my legs.

"Bishop," I moan, and he lets out a groan as he wraps his lips around the stiff peak.

I can feel his beard rubbing against my sensitive skin and it only heightens my arousal. He switches back and forth between my breasts, and I gasp, moan, and arch against him.

"More," I beg, growing more and more frustrated.

He nods, kissing his way down my body as he settles between my thighs. I have a moment of self-conscience as he comes face to face with my core.

"You're so fucking wet, baby," he groans as he uses two of his fingers to spread my pussy lips.

I look down and see his dark head moving closer and then his mouth is on me. My eyes fall closed, and I fist the sheets as he uses his mouth to drive me higher and higher.

His thumb rolls over my clit, and my hips shoot off the bed.

"Bishop!" I scream as his hand pins me back to the bed.

He sucks the little pearl in his mouth, and I scream again as my orgasm comes barreling towards me.

I come hard, my thighs clamping down around his head as my back arches off of the mattress. My fingers tangle in his dark locks, and I scream his name as I come against his mouth.

"Bishop!" I sob as he continues to lick me through my orgasm.

I tremble as my body sags back against the bed, and he kisses the inside of each of my thighs and then makes his way up my body. I'm still mostly limp as he claims my mouth with his. I can taste my release on his lips, and I moan at the tangy flavor.

"Are you ready for me?" He asks, and I nod eagerly, spreading my legs wider in invitation.

I should tell him.

"Wait!" I shout, my head bracing against his chest and he stops instantly.

"We don't have to do anything, baby," he promises me, ready to roll to the side, but I stop him.

"No, I want you! I just wanted to tell you something."

"What's that?"

"I'm... a virgin," I admit and he smiles down at me.

"Good."

"Good?"

"Yeah. I like that you'll be all mine. Just like I'm all yours."

I want to ask him if that means that he's also a virgin, but before I can, his lips are on mine and I forget about everything but what he's doing to me.

I moan as his cock brushes against my opening, and we both look down and watch as he starts to push inside of me.

The tip barely fits inside of me, and I hold my breath as he pushes in an inch and then another inch. He stops when he bumps up against my virginity, and I look up, meeting his dark blue eyes. I nod at him, and he leans down and kisses me as he thrusts forward, popping my cherry and claiming me as his.

I cry out at the sting of pain, and he kisses me, one hand moving to play with my breast as he starts to move inside of me.

"Oh!" I gasp as the pain fades and pleasure blossoms in its place.

"Fuck, baby. God, Alba, you feel so good. So tight. So perfect."

His words have tingles spreading throughout my body,

and I grip his biceps, my nails biting into his skin there as another orgasm starts to build inside of me.

"I'm close," I pant, and Bishop nods, his pace picking up until he's pounding into me.

His cock brushes against my clit with each thrust, and I moan, my body tightening deliciously as I start to come.

"Bishop!" I scream, my voice cutting out halfway through as my mind blanks.

All I feel is pleasure and Bishop coming deep inside of me. I blink my eyes open, wanting to see him reach his own peak. He's so handsome; his tan skin flushed a pale pink as he finds his release and moans my name.

His dark blue eyes meet mine, and he grins down at me for a second before his lips find mine.

"Whoa," I breathe, and I have to clear my throat.

"I see that you're not quite hoarse yet," he says in a husky voice.

"Not yet," I agree and he grins as he bows his head and kisses me.

I stay wrapped around him for half the night, and it takes another three orgasms before I pass out. True to his word, though, by the time Bishop is done with me, I'm hoarse, and I know I'll be sore for the next few days.

It's totally worth it, though.

<h1 style="text-align:center">SEVEN</h1>

Bishop

WHEN I WAKE up the next morning with Alba's hot little mouth wrapped around my cock, I think that I'm dreaming. I mean, being with her like this is literally a dream come true. Then she looks up at me, mischief and need swirling in her blue eyes, and I blink, realizing that it's not a dream.

"Fuck, baby," I groan as she sucks on my cock.

"Good morning," she says with a giggle.

"What a good, good morning," I say, and she giggles again.

"I figured that it was only fair since you got to taste me last night."

"You can taste me anytime you want," I pant as she goes back to licking and sucking my cock.

Her hand wraps around my length and she jerks me off in time with her mouth. My thighs tense, and I watch as her head bobs up and down on my length.

"Fuck, Alba, you're so good at this, baby."

She moans around my length, and I know that I'm close to coming.

"Come here. I need you," I plead with her, and she shakes her head.

"I want you to come in my mouth."

Her words almost have me coming, and I grit my teeth.

"I want to make you come too," I say, and she smiles.

"Later."

She wraps her mouth around my cock and sucks hard. I groan, cursing under my breath and I know that I won't be able to hold out for too much longer.

"Alba... Alba!" I shout, tapping her arm twice to warn her that I'm about to come.

She sucks and moans in response. I come a second later, and Alba swallows around me, her hand rubbing my length, milking every drop of come out of me.

"Fuck," I moan, and she smiles as she kisses my stomach, and then she trails kisses up my body.

"You didn't have to do that," I tell her as I catch my breath.

"I wanted to," she insists. "I like taking care of you."

My heart swells in my chest. That's my girl. Alba is just as lonely as I am. I think that's what I recognized on the day that I hired her. We were both looking for our other half and I'm so happy that she found my flyer and came in for it.

"My turn," I say as I roll her under me.

She giggles as I spread her legs. My hand dips between us, and I curse when I feel how wet she is.

"Did sucking my cock make you this wet?" I ask her, and she nods.

"I love making you feel good. Hearing the sounds you made. The way that you said my name."

I can't wait any longer to have her, and I know she's

ready for me. I spread Alba's legs, and we both moan as I thrust into her.

"So tight," I grit out as I start to fuck her.

"So big," she moans back.

I brace my hands on either side of her head and kiss her lightly before I kiss her neck and then down to her breasts. I lick a path down to one nipple and then take the little cherry into my mouth to tease.

"Oh!" She gasps as I scrape my teeth over the sensitive bud.

"Love hearing the sounds that you make," I groan.

Her hands tangle in my hair, and she holds me against her as I switch to her other breast and give it the same attention.

I can feel her pussy starting to tighten around my length, and I know that she's close to coming. I want to feel that, want to feel her juices coating me as she comes all over my cock. I want to hear her scream my name again.

"Oh, oh, oh!" She says as her eyes fall closed.

A flush stains her cheeks, and I reach between us, pinching her clit and sending her flying over the edge.

"Bishop!" She screams, and hearing her say my name like that has me following her over the edge.

I come with her, and we both collapse on the bed, trying to catch our breaths. My alarm goes off a minute later, and I groan as I silence it.

"Time to get up?" Alba asks me, and I nod.

"Unfortunately. I want nothing more than to stay in bed with you all day."

She gives me a smile, and I kiss her lips before I pull myself out of bed. I hate to wash her scent off me, so I just pull on my clothes and get ready for my day.

Alba is still in bed, looking flushed and cozy. I hate to

leave her, but I know I have to get to the job site to help out today.

"I have to go to work," I say apologetically, and she nods.

"I know. I should get to work, too. My boss is a real grump," she teases me, and I grin.

"Why don't you take today off?" I suggest.

"Maybe."

"Don't forget about our date and tour tonight," I remind her, and she grins.

"I won't."

I kiss her goodbye, taking one last longing look at her before I head for the door. I'm already counting down the minutes until I can come home and join her in that bed again.

EIGHT

Alba

WHEN MY PHONE RINGS, I'm expecting it to be Bishop checking in on me or maybe calling to tell me that he's headed home. Instead, when I look at the screen, I see Elizabeth, my old roommate's name there.

"Hey!" I greet her as I answer.

"Hey, how's it going?" She asks, her nasally voice reminding me of all of our nights spent wandering around San Francisco.

"Pretty good. What about you? How's the big city?"

"It's good, the same," she says.

"Are you stuck in traffic?" I ask when I hear a car horn honk in the background.

"Of course," she sighs, and I smile slightly.

"I don't miss that."

"I bet! Where are you right now?"

"It's this small town in Oregon called Clearwater. It's really cute," I tell her. "Plus, no traffic ever."

"Brag. I would take a small town right about now."

"How have you been?" I ask as I settle onto the couch.

"Pretty good. Everything is basically the same as when you left. I met someone. He's a tech guy. Things are still new, but I really like him," she says.

I'm not surprised. Elizabeth always had a boyfriend or a new guy. She always really liked them, too... for the first few weeks. Then she would get bored and be onto the next guy.

"Yeah? That's cool. I met someone too," I admit, and I know that will be a shock to her since I have never dated before.

"Really? Who is the lucky guy?"

"His name is Bishop. He owns a construction company here in town," I tell her.

"Ohh, is he hot?" She asks.

"So hot," I gush, grinning to myself.

"Hot and successful! You hit the jackpot."

"I really did," I agree.

"How did you two meet?" She asks, and I could swear that I can hear a note of jealousy in her voice.

I brush that off as I think about first meeting Bishop.

"I went to his office to apply for a job. He hired me to be his housekeeper and secretary for his company."

"Oh! So you're like a gold digger," Elizabeth says, and my stomach drops.

"What?"

"I mean, you're with him for stability, a job, and money," she points out, and my throat feels like it's starting to close up.

A gold digger? No, that's not what I am. I mean, I was going to take a job working for his company, and he was the one who offered me the housekeeper job. I didn't weasel my way into his life or try to seduce him. I was just being me. We just like each other.

Right?

"I didn't know that you had it in you," Elizabeth says, sounding like she's proud of me for being a gold digger.

I want to tell her that I'm not, and even if I was, it wouldn't be something to be proud of, but I can't seem to get the words out. I can't seem to do much of anything except sit here, my mind running away with all different ideas.

Doubts are starting to pile up inside of me as Elizabeth starts to tell me all about her new man and roommate. I'm starting to see that Elizabeth was never really my friend. She probably just hung out with me because I wasn't a threat. I wasn't going to steal her man of the moment or show her up in any way. I just made her feel better about herself.

I hit end on the call and throw my phone to the side. I'm not sure when I started crying, but I sniffle, brushing at the tears as I look around Bishop's house.

Gold digger.

I can't stop thinking about it now. I'm not. I'm not after Bishop for his money or anything. I know that, but I can't help but wonder what Bishop thinks. Is he just using me because I'm here and convenient? I know how busy he is, so maybe he just doesn't have time to date, and I'm making it easy for him to have all of his needs met.

I choke on a sob and close my eyes, wondering what the heck I should do now.

NINE

Bishop

COMING HOME USED to just be another part of my boring routine. Now that I have Alba there waiting for me, though, I can't wait to get back.

Today might actually be the first time since I started Clearwater Construction that I left before five o'clock. I wanted to get home and shower so that I had enough time to get ready before our date tonight. I've been planning out my tour of town all day, and I'm excited to show it to Alba.

I used to kind of hate this town too, but I think that maybe those feelings were just tied to my parents and growing up here with them. When I actually thought about it, Clearwater had a lot of cool things that I think my girl will like.

I park next to her old car and smile. I went down on my lunch break today and got her a new one. They had to bring it in from one of their dealerships nearby, but it should be delivered to the house tomorrow. I can't wait to see Alba's face when it gets here.

I hop out of my truck and head up to the front door, smiling as I make my way inside. The house smells like lemons, and I know that Alba was busy cleaning because the place is spotless.

Maybe I should talk to her about that. She doesn't have to cook or clean if she doesn't want to. We can hire someone, and she can spend her days doing stuff that she's actually interested in. Maybe I can check the classes at the community center and see if she wants to do any of them.

I smile at the thought as I set my boots next to her shoes and head off to find my girl. She's not in the kitchen or office, so I head upstairs. I find her in her room and at first, I think that she's packing up her things to move into my room. I'm about to offer to help, when I realize she's sliding her packed bag under the bed and not moving it anywhere.

"Hey, going somewhere?" I ask, trying not to panic.

"Hey, how was work?" She asks with a tired smile.

"Good. How was your day?" I ask.

I'm studying her because she seems off. She's acting distant, and she looks sad. I wrack my brain, trying to figure out what could have happened between this morning and now to upset her.

Maybe she's just tired. I kept her up late last night, after all.

I try to convince myself that that's all this is as I offer her my hand and help her to her feet.

"Ready for our date and the tour?" I ask her, and she gives me a weak smile.

"We don't have to go out. I can make us something here," she says, and I frown.

Does she not want to go out on a date with me?

"Are you feeling alright?"

I raise my hand to check her forehead for a fever, but she doesn't feel warm to me.

"I'm fine," she says, pulling away from me.

"Did something happen? I thought that you were excited for tonight."

"I was—I am!" She corrects, and panic starts to settle in my gut.

"What's going on, Alba?" I ask.

I need her to tell me what's wrong so that I can fix it, but she shakes her head and gives me a forced smile.

"Nothing. I'm fine," she insists. "When did you want to leave?"

"I just need to take a shower and change."

She nods, and I pause. I want to push this issue and make her tell me what has upset her and why she's being so distant with me, but I don't want to be overbearing or make her more upset so I let it go.

"I'll be ready in a few," I tell her, and she nods again, not meeting my eyes.

I hate it, but I turn to head into my own room to get ready.

I'll make sure that this is the best date ever. Then she'll be in a better mood. Then she'll be happy and we can talk about what was wrong then.

I rush through my shower and pull on a nice button-down shirt and a pair of newer, dark-wash jeans. There's nothing super fancy in Clearwater. Most restaurants are relaxed, laid-back places and not formal.

I head back to find Alba, and she's standing in her room, looking around like she's trying to memorize the room to memory. Something is definitely wrong, but I decide to stick to my plan and make tonight great for her.

"Ready to go?" I ask her gently, and she starts, turning to face me with a smile pasted on her lips.

"Yeah. You look nice."

"Thanks, so do you."

She does. She's wearing a light purple sweater and a pair of skinny jeans that show off her curves and have me desperate to grab and hold her against me.

She heads past me and I follow her downstairs and over to my truck. I open her door for her and glance over at her car as she climbs into the passenger seat. I wonder if I should tell her about the new car. Maybe it would help brighten her mood a bit. I decide to wait and see if just getting out of the house helps before I surprise her with that.

We head into town, and I reach over and take her hand in mine as we drive toward downtown. It's still early, so the streets are pretty empty.

"Are you hungry right now, or do you want to drive around for a bit?" I ask her.

"I'm not that hungry," she says softly.

I don't like this timid, sad version of Alba. I want my clumsy, optimistic girl back who isn't afraid to be herself.

"Okay, I'll give you the grand tour first, then," I say, smiling as I squeeze her hand in mine.

She smiles back slightly, and I turn away from downtown and head towards the lake. Clearwater Lake is just outside of town and is where the town got its name.

"This is the lake," I tell Alba as we head down the slightly bumpy dirt road that leads to the water. "There's a few camping sites around it."

Alba is looking out the window and she seems to like the water.

"Do you like camping?" I ask her, and she shrugs.

"I don't know. I never went. I think my parents were kind of afraid to take me hiking or out camping since I was liable to trip over a rock or a root or something and hurt myself."

"I'll keep you safe," I promise her.

She just keeps looking out at the water. I park in one of the small lots and turn to her.

"Did you want to get out and go for a walk?" I offer, and she bites her bottom lip, debating before she shakes her head.

"Not today."

She still seems glum, and I search my brain for somewhere else to show her to cheer her up.

"Okay, let's head back to town. I can show you some of my old haunts."

We drive back down the dirt road, and I turn and head towards Fisher's old place.

"This was my best friend's house," I say, pointing to the old house.

"Fisher, right?" She asks, and I nod.

I forgot that I had mentioned him a few times in passing. I like that she remembers. It means that she's been listening and paying attention to me the same way that I've been paying attention to her.

"Yeah, that was Fisher's house and that right there is where I grew up."

My stomach twists and cramps as I stare at the rundown house. It never looked like much, but the years have only made it worse.

"It looks small," Alba comments. "It's hard to believe that you would even fit through the door."

She giggles and I smile as I stare at the small front door that looks like a soft kick could knock it off the frame.

"I wasn't always this big."

"Really? When did you have your growth spurt?"

"I was a late bloomer. I was probably fifteen or sixteen when I really had my big growth spurt."

We drive down the quiet street and I turn onto Main Street. People are starting to head home so there are a few cars on the roads. We stop at a red light, and I see Alba taking in all of the little shops that line the street.

"Any stores that you want to go check out? We could get some stuff for the house," I offer and she shakes her head.

"No, that's okay."

"Should we grab dinner?" I ask her, and she shakes her head.

"I'm not really hungry. We can just go back to the house."

She sounds so solemn, and I'm at my limit. I need to fix this. I need to see my girl smile. I turn to head back to the house and rub my thumb back and forth across her palm as we go.

"I have a surprise for you," I tell her as I turn onto our street.

She looks over at me, and I grin as I pull into the driveway.

"I bought you a new car," I tell her.

I'm expecting a smile or excitement. Instead, at my words, Alba bursts into tears next to me.

I go into panic mode, shutting the truck off and reaching for her. I unbuckle her seatbelt and pull her over the center console and into my lap. I wrap her up tight in my arms and do my best to comfort her.

"What's wrong, baby? Just tell me and I'll fix it," I promise her.

She sobs in my arms, and I start to really panic.

What could be wrong? What could have possibly happened to upset her this much?

"I have to leave," she says between sobs, and I freeze.

"Why the hell would you do that?" I demand to know, pulling back so that I can see her face.

She sniffles, looking up at me with those pretty blue eyes. I hold my breath, waiting to hear what's wrong so I can come up with a plan to make it right.

TEN

Alba

IT FEELS SO good to be in Bishop's arms. I want to remember this because I know I probably won't have it for very long. Being around Bishop without actually being with him will kill me, and I know that when he gets tired of me, I'll have to move on. That's why I was packing my things when he got home. I wasn't expecting him to be back so soon, and I thought I would have more time to get my head on straight and try to hide my heartbreak.

When he walked in, I knew that I was screwed and was going to fall apart soon. I had tried to tell him that he didn't need to take me out. I didn't want him to spend any more money on me, but he seemed so excited to go, and I didn't want to let him down.

All of my insecurities were building in me and when he told me he had bought me a new car, I just couldn't hold it in any longer. I don't want to talk about the end of our relationship, though. I just want to try to pretend that everything is okay for a little bit longer.

"Why are you talking about leaving?" Bishop asks me.

I can't tell if he sounds more worried or mad when he asks, and I sniffle, wiping at my tears.

"What's going on, Alba? You have to tell me, baby."

I look away from his dark blue eyes and take a deep breath.

"I talked to Elizabeth today," I start.

"Who?"

"My old roommate. She lived with me in the apartment that caught on fire."

"Okay. Is she alright?"

"Yeah, she's fine. She just... said something."

"Said what?" He asks impatiently.

"She called me a gold digger," I whisper.

Bishop's whole body goes tense and he looks pissed. I start to pull back from him, worried that he's mad at me, but Bishop tightens his hold on me, keeping me in place.

"First of all, I don't want you talking to Elizabeth anymore. She sounds like an idiot and a bad friend."

My mouth drops open, but I have no words.

"Secondly, you're not a gold digger. How could you be? You're working for your money and I haven't even paid you yet!" He exclaims and I pause to think about his words.

He's right.

"Did you know I had money when you walked into the Clearwater Construction offices?" He demands to know, and I shake my head.

"No, you were just the only one in town that was hiring," I swear to him.

"Okay, so how are you a gold digger? You didn't flirt with me. I kissed you first. You haven't asked me to buy you anything. In fact, you bought groceries. If you're a gold digger, you're not very good at it."

I giggle at that, and he smiles.

"Why are you with me, baby? Is it for my money?"

"No, I just like you. You're sweet and you make me laugh. I like making you smile and taking care of you. You make me feel safe and pretty. I just... feel like myself around you."

"Me too, baby. Me too."

He pulls me against him and I relax as his arms wrap around my waist.

"I think your old roommate is a terrible friend. She's putting dumb things in your head that just aren't true. Even if they were, I wouldn't care. I love you, Alba. I want you forever. You can have all of my money as long as you give me your heart in return."

Tears sting my eyes again, and I wrap my arms around his neck and cling to him.

"I don't want your money. Just your heart," I tell him as he pulls me tighter against him. "I love you too, Bishop."

"Why didn't you just tell me? I want to know when you're upset or having doubts so I can handle them and reassure you."

"I was scared that maybe you would think that I was using you," I admit, and he squeezes my waist.

"You're not like that," he tells me. "You're sweet and good, Alba. I trust you. I love you."

"I love you too," I say, and he grins at me.

I smile back up at him and the next second, his lips are claiming mine. Heat blooms inside me, and all I can think about is Bishop claiming me again.

I want that, to be with him, to have him make love to me.

I need him.

"Alba, baby," Bishop groans as he cups my face in his hands, and I smile as I hear the longing in his voice.

I know at that moment that everything is going to be okay.

ELEVEN

Bishop

I PULL Alba flush against me, and we both groan at the contact. It feels like it's been forever since we were last intimate, even though it was only just this morning.

"I need you," she whispers to me, and I nod.

"I've got you. I love you," I tell her as I push back the seat of my truck to make room for both of us.

"Here?" Alba whispers, looking around outside.

There's no one and nothing for at least a mile, and I grin at her.

"I need you. I can't wait," I tell her, and I can tell that she likes my words.

She nods eagerly, and we move quickly, both of us working to get the other out of their clothes. Alba laughs as we shove her pants and underwear down to her knees.

"Wait," she says, gasping as she tips over into the passenger seat and pushes one leg out of her pants. "There."

"Come back over here," I tell her as I push my pants down to my knees.

She straddles me again, and I hold her hips and help her lower down onto my length.

"Fuck," we both hiss at the same time.

Alba closes her eyes and tips forward. I laugh as I right her and help her find her rhythm as she moves on top of me.

"It's so deep this way," she moans, and I nod.

"So good."

She nods, her hands gripping my shoulders as she uses them for leverage as she rides me. Her tits bounce in front of my face, and I lean forward, burying my face between the soft mounds.

My hands slide under her shirt, and I find her nipples, rolling the peaks between my fingers.

"Bishop!" She gasps, and I pinch them harder.

She rides me faster, and I can feel my balls tighten up as pleasure builds inside of me. I'm close to coming, and I know I need to get my girl off first.

I reach between us, finding her clit and rolling the bundle of nerves under my thumb. Alba arches against me, her pussy tightening around my length. I grab the back of her neck with my other hand, pulling her forward until our mouths crash together.

As soon as I slip my tongue into her mouth, she comes, moaning, her grip on my shoulders tightening as she finds her release and takes me with her over the edge.

She pants, sagging against me, and I catch her, rubbing her back as we both come down from our highs.

"I love you, Bishop," she tells me, and I nod.

"I love you, baby."

She starts to climb off of me, and her elbow bangs against the horn, and we both startle and then laugh.

"We should have gone inside. Car sex isn't as much fun as I thought that it would be," she says with a laugh.

"I'm too big for it, I think."

My phone starts to ring, and I glance at the screen as I pull my clothes back on.

"Who is it?" Alba asks.

"My friend, Fisher."

She rights her clothes, and I lean over, kissing her. I climb out of the truck and answer the phone as I head over to help my girl out.

"Hey," I answer.

"Hey, are you home?" He asks me.

"Yeah, just got back. Why? Are you in the area?"

"Yeah, I'm right up the road. I was hoping to stop in and talk to you."

"Sure. Come on over."

I hang up and take Alba's hand in mine.

"He's coming for a visit," I tell her, and she smiles.

"Cool. It will be nice to meet one of your oldest friends. Do you think he'll tell me embarrassing stories about you if I ask?" She asks with a giggle.

"Maybe... if there were any embarrassing stories about me," I tell her, and she laughs.

I take her hand in mine as we head for the front door. I'm unlocking the front door when a car pulls in next to my truck, and I turn to see Fisher climbing out of his car.

"That was fast," I comment.

"I was literally right up the road."

He heads my way, and we hug briefly.

"It's good to see you," I tell him.

"You too. Who is this?"

"This is Alba, my girlfriend."

Girlfriend doesn't seem like a strong enough word, and I vow to make her my wife soon enough.

"Ah, the fire starter," Fisher says with a grin, and Alba blushes.

"You told him!?"

"I... might have," I admit, and she swats at my arm.

"It's nice to meet you," Alba says, and Fisher nods.

"You too."

"Well, I'll let you two talk. I'll be inside."

"See you," Fisher tells her and she waves before she heads into the house.

"What are you doing in town?" I ask him.

"I was in the area."

"You hate this area," I point out."

"I was curious about how this thing was working out," he says, nodding to where Alba just was.

"It's going good. Really good."

He nods, chewing on his lip. He looks deep in thought, and I frown.

"I love her," I tell him, and he smiles.

"Good. I'm glad for you two."

"What's going on, Fisher?"

"I met someone," he sighs, and my eyebrows rise.

"Who? Where?"

"She lives and works in Wolf Valley."

"Oh, so you met her when you went to start your resort."

"Kind of. She's... well, she's preventing me from building the resort."

"How?"

"She owns the land but doesn't want to sell."

"Okay, so find a different spot."

"I know, that's not my problem."

"What is then?" I ask him.

"I want her. I just don't know how to make her mine, especially not after I pissed her off."

"Well, I'm no expert, but I would start by apologizing."

"Yeah, I've tried that. It's not going well."

"Try harder," I say with a shrug.

"You're a wealth of wisdom and knowledge," he says drily, and I laugh.

"Sorry, man. I just lucked out."

"You are lucky," he sighs, and I nod.

"I know."

We're silent for a minute, and then he turns to me.

"You want to come in for a drink or something?" I ask him, and he shakes his head.

"No, I'll let you have some alone time with your girl. I should get back to mine and try to fix things."

"Good luck."

"Thanks. I'll talk to you soon."

We hug goodbye, and I wave as he drives off down the road.

I head inside and smile when I see Alba in the kitchen.

"Is Fisher staying for dinner?" She asks, and I shake my head.

"He just left."

"Oh, that's too bad."

"We'll hang out with him a different time."

"What did you want to have for dinner then?" She asks. I grab her elbow and turn her to face me.

"Why don't we order something?" I ask as I duck my head and kiss her neck.

"Sure. What should we do while we wait for the food?" She asks in a husky whisper.

"I've got a few ideas," I tell her with a grin, and she smirks back at me.

"Yeah? Why don't you tell me a few?"

"I'd rather show you."

"Even better," she murmurs, and I grin as go about doing just that.

TWELVE

Alba

FIVE YEARS LATER...

"ARE you excited for Daddy to come home?" I coo at my son and he gurgles up at me.

I smile, grabbing his little hands in mine as he kicks his chubby legs and babbles up at me.

"He's going to be so excited when he sees you can roll over now!"

Benson smiles up at me, his blue eyes sparkling as he stares up at me. We're laying on his tummy time mat, and he's happy to kick his legs and babble at me.

Bishop is still running Clearwater Construction, though he's stepped back from some of his duties and hired a few more employees to help out. I'm still working as his assistant, though I have worked from home ever since

Benson was born. Bishop's home office has become mine over the last five years.

We got married six months after we met. We had a small ceremony here in Clearwater with just our closest friends. I met Bishop's best friend, Fisher, and we hung out for longer than a minute. Then a month after our wedding, we were at his wedding to his wife, Vera. The two of us have gotten close over the last few years, and we see them often since they're just down the road in Wolf Valley.

Bishop and I waited a few years before we started trying to have kids. Bishop said he wanted to have all of my attention for a while, and I was fine with that since I wanted all of his as well. We spent the first few years traveling and just enjoying being together. Bishop signed up for a few classes at the community center in town with me, though none of them seemed to be his cup of tea. I was just happy that he was going with me, and it was fun to see him trying to learn how to crotchet or do needlepoint.

We started trying for a baby close to two years ago and found out that we were expecting after a few months. Benson was born just after the New Year, and he's been the light of our life ever since.

Benson is such a happy, easy baby that it has me ready for another already. Well, sometimes. Some days, I love that it's just the three of us and that we can give our son all of our attention, and some days, I get baby fever and want to give him a sibling.

I hear my husband's truck pull up out front, and I grin down at Benson in excitement.

"Daddy is home!" I tell him, and he kicks his legs and flails his arms in excitement.

I look up as the front door opens and smile as Bishop comes inside.

"There are my two favorite people," he says as he kicks off his shoes and hurries over to us.

He lays down on his stomach next to me, leaning over to kiss me before he greets our son.

"How is my little guy?" He asks him gently.

Benson gurgles up at him and Bishop grins down at him. The two look so much alike. Benson got his dad's dark blue eyes and brown hair. I know that he's going to be just as big as his dad too. He's already in the ninetieth percentile for his height and weight and he's only four months old.

"Guess what our little one did today?" I ask Bishop, and he looks over at me.

"What's that? Besides being the most adorable baby ever."

"He rolled over!" I tell him and his eyes widen.

"No way! That's so good, little man!"

Benson screeches, and we both laugh.

"Let's see if we can show Daddy," I tell our son as I help him roll over onto his stomach.

Almost immediately, his chunky little body twists and he rolls back over onto his back. Bishop cheers, and Benson screeches again, gurgling and giggling as he squirms on the mat.

"You're so smart," Bishop says as he tickles his stomach. "Just like your mama."

I lean over and kiss his cheek before I push to my knees.

"Dinner should be ready soon," I tell him as I head for the kitchen.

"It smells good."

"It's your favorite!" I call back to him.

"Chicken tetrazzini?" He asks excitedly.

"Of course."

He grins and starts telling Benson how good it is. I add

the biscuits to the oven and set the timer. I see Bishop pick Benson up, cradling him against his chest and carrying him upstairs. He must need a new diaper.

I set the table, setting up Benson's high chair between us. He's not eating solids yet, but he loves to play with his toys while we eat.

The timer goes off and I take out the food as Bishop comes back in and sets Benson up in his high chair.

"Looks great, baby."

I smile as we take our seats. I never thought that I would meet a man I'd fall in love with. I never thought that I would get married or have kids, but I do, and it's all because I wandered into Bishop's construction company looking for a job. I might not have gotten the position, but in the end, I got a better one. As Bishop's wife and partner.

I smile at him as we both dig in.

WANT A FREE BOOK?

***You can grab Sweets* Here.**
**Check out my website, www.shawhart.com for
more free books!**

ABOUT THE AUTHOR

CONNECT WITH ME!

If you enjoyed this story, please consider leaving a review on Amazon or any other reader site or blog that you like. Don't forget to recommend it to your other reader friends.

If you want to chat with me, please consider joining my VIP list or connecting with me on one of my Social Media platforms. I love talking with each of my readers. Links below!

<u>Website</u>
<u>Newsletter</u>

A Very Mountain Man New Year

Folklore
Kidnapping His Forever

Claiming His Forever

Finding His Forever

Rescuing His Forever

Chasing His Forever

Folklore: The Complete Series

Holiday Hearts
Be Mine

Falling in Love

Holly Jolly Holidays

Love Notes
Signing Off With Love

Care Package Love

Wrong Number, Right Love

Kings Gym
Fighting Fire With Fire

Fighting Tooth and Nail

Fighting Back From Hell

Mine To
Mine to Love

Mine to Protect

Mine to Cherish

<u>Mine to Keep</u>

Mine to: The Complete Series

<u>Sequoia: Stud Farm</u>

Branded

Bucked

Roped

Spurred

<u>Sequoia: Fast Love Racing</u>

Jump Start

Pit Stop

Home Stretch

<u>Telltale Heart</u>

<u>Bought and Paid For</u>

<u>His Miracle</u>

<u>Pretty Girl</u>

<u>Telltale Hearts Boxset</u>

ALSO BY SHAW HART

Still in the mood for Christmas books?

Stuffing Her Stocking, Mistletoe Kisses, Snowed in For Christmas,
Coming Down Her Chimney

Love holiday books? Check out these!

For Better or Worse, Riding His Broomstick, Thankful for His
FAKE Girlfriend, His New Year Resolution, Hop Stuff, Taming
Her Beast, Hungry For Dash, His Firework

Looking for some OTT love stories?

Her Scottish Savior, Baby Mama, Tempted By My Roommate,
Blame It On The Rum, Wild Ride, Always

Looking for a celebrity love story?

Bedroom Eyes, Seducing Archer, Finding Their Rhythm

In the mood for some young love books?

Study Dates, His Forever, My Girl

Some other books by Shaw:

The Billionaire's Bet, Her Guardian Angel, Falling Again,
Stealing Her, Dreamboat, Making Her His, Trouble

www.ingramcontent.com/pod-product-compliance
Lightning Source LLC
Chambersburg PA
CBHW051808130726
47987CB00003B/1169